To

From

With thanks to
Annie Simpson and Karen Morrison

Copyright © 2009

make believe ideas

27 Castle Street, Berkhamsted,
Hertfordshire, HP4 2DW.

Manufactured in China

10 Little PENGUINS

KATE TOMS

make
believe
ideas

eady for some fun . . .

ay before the day's begun.

earch me!

1 penguin eats too fast and now has tummy ache!

Oh dear!

6 happy penguins, al

5 quiet penguins watch

but **1** has seen this one befor

...heir favorite show . . .

...nd thinks it's time to go.

4 hungry penguins are

1 cries, "Not sardines!" and jump

Salt

funny penguins ar

kating 'round and 'round . . .

1 tries

a somersault

and crashes

to the ground!

smelly penguins take

Tee hee
Tee hee

tired little penguin

She thought her friends